DEDICATION

I would like to dedicate this book to my dear family, who have always given me the happiness necessary to create: my husband, Helmut Hofmeister; my children, Amanda and Jason; my grandchildren, Silver, Chevala, and Cyrus; and of course my parents, Bob and Nancy Simpson.

The First Beaver

Written and Illustrated
by Caroll Simpson

VANCOUVER • VICTORIA • CALGARY

In the olden days, before
you were born, the arms of
Mother Earth embraced a
valley with mammoth cedar
trees. The music of falling
water and the song of the
red-winged blackbird echoed
in the giant forest.

The animals watched the First People as
they built their longhouses. Food was
plentiful, and the people were happy.

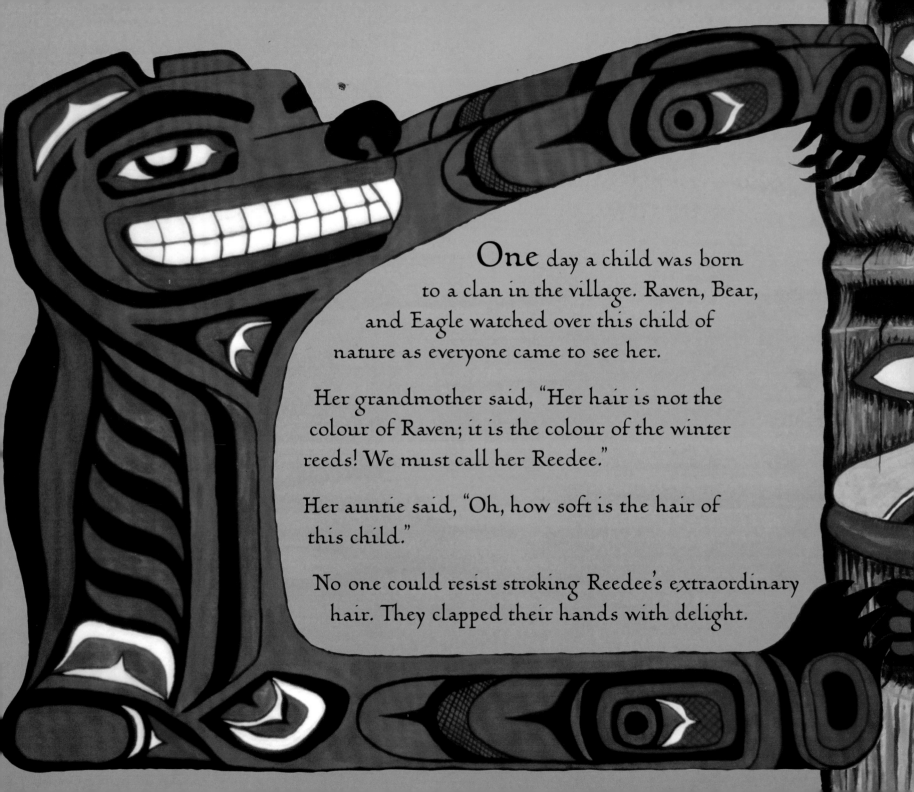

One day a child was born
to a clan in the village. Raven, Bear,
and Eagle watched over this child of
nature as everyone came to see her.

Her grandmother said, "Her hair is not the
colour of Raven; it is the colour of the winter
reeds! We must call her Reedee."

Her auntie said, "Oh, how soft is the hair of
this child."

No one could resist stroking Reedee's extraordinary
hair. They clapped their hands with delight.

As Reedee grew, it was not just her beautiful hair that was different. The First People worked by the light from the sun and the fire. At night, everyone slept—everyone except Reedee! When darkness fell, she disappeared into the forest.

"Where does she go?" Reedee's mother asked her husband. Her parents wanted Reedee to fit in and be happy.

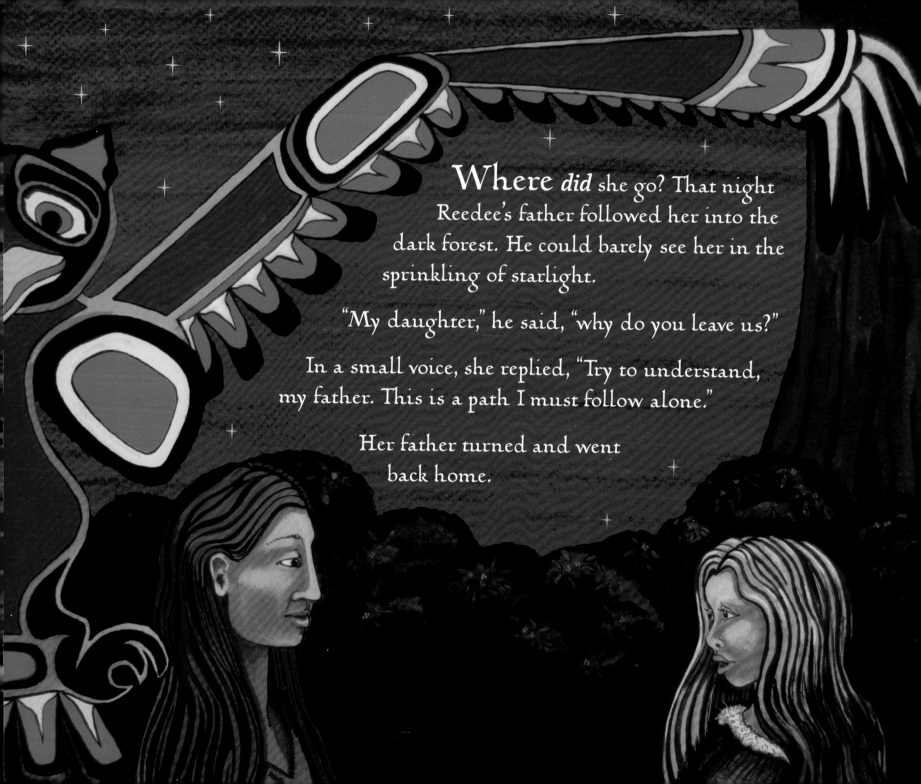

Where *did* she go? That night Reedee's father followed her into the dark forest. He could barely see her in the sprinkling of starlight.

"My daughter," he said, "why do you leave us?"

In a small voice, she replied, "Try to understand, my father. This is a path I must follow alone."

Her father turned and went back home.

The next evening, Reedee overheard a great discussion. The elders were concerned.

"No music rises from the creek, and no birds sing," they said.

"The women walk far to find water for our families," they complained.

Reedee went into the forest earlier and earlier from that night on.

The next morning, a large basket of berries, a basket of water, and stacks of firewood surrounded the sleeping Reedee. Her parents could smell smoked salmon in the air. They wanted to ask her where she had gone, but they could not wake her.

As the creek dried up, Reedee spent more and more time in the dark forest. She would come home exhausted and fall into a deep sleep.

"Why does she go into the forest?" her mother cried.

Night after night Reedee's father paced the floor, worrying about his daughter. But he waited for the next full moon before he followed her again. Her shining hair was easy to see in the moonlight. Even so, suddenly she vanished.

Her father peered
into the dark, looking
for her. The creek was gone.
A lake opened in front of him.

He called to his daughter.

Only the music of the night replied: frogs
croaked, bugs **buzzed**, and the loon called out.
Reedee's father followed the shore and found
a dam blocking the creek. He searched
through the fireweed and the cattails,
in a panic to find his daughter.

Finally, he went back to the village.

"Reedee is nowhere to be found,"
he told his wife.

The next morning, Reedee's bed was still empty.

Her parents were awoken by music. They ran outside to see what was happening. The people had put their leather work aprons away. They had taken their drums and hats off the walls. They had taken their button blankets from their special storage boxes. They wore their ceremonial clothing proudly.

All the First People sang songs of water.
"It is a miracle," they said.

But Reedee's parents missed their daughter. They walked back to their lodge, slowly. There inside, Reedee was fast asleep!

That night her mother tried to keep her daughter home. But light from the moon cast shadows through the smoke hole, and Reedee's mother became spellbound by the smoke and moonbeams. She dreamed of her daughter swimming in the moonlight. Reedee smiled as she swam. Joy filled her mother's heart.

When Reedee's mother awoke the next morning, a button blanket lay on her daughter's bed, but Reedee was gone.

Reedee's father went back to the lake that night. He called out her name.

"Reedee, Reedeeeee!"

Reedee heard her father, but her voice had become too small to answer. She **slapped** her tail on the water, and a huge **bang** filled the air. Her father jumped back and fell into the lake. His moccasin lace hooked on a stick deep underwater. He struggled to free it.

Then, right beside him, Reedee spoke quietly. "Father, please do not be frightened." He stopped struggling, and his lace came free.

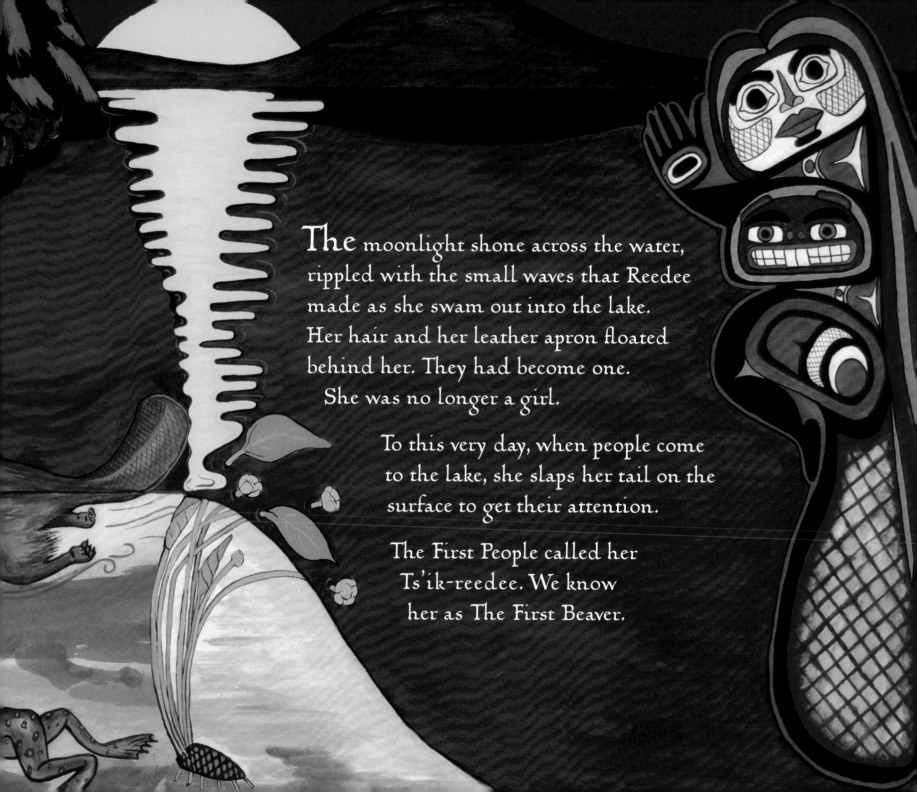

The moonlight shone across the water, rippled with the small waves that Reedee made as she swam out into the lake. Her hair and her leather apron floated behind her. They had become one. She was no longer a girl.

To this very day, when people come to the lake, she slaps her tail on the surface to get their attention.

The First People called her Ts'ik-reedee. We know her as The First Beaver.

Crests

Crests are stylized images of animals, birds, people, and supernatural beings. Crests are symbols that identify the members of a clan.

A clan is a group of families with the same ancestors. Clan members share crests and legends about their clan history. A clan member could inherit crests, acquire them through marriage, or receive them for achievement.

A clan holds a potlatch to proclaim ownership of and to gain acceptance for a new crest.

Crests adorn hats, homes, boxes, baskets, blankets, totem poles, clothes, and dishes. First Peoples even tattooed crests on their bodies.

Bear

A bear crest shows a large mouth full of teeth, including two large canine teeth; a tongue, sticking out; flared nostrils; ears; and paws with claws. Bear crests often show a mother bear with two cubs or a male bear with a human wife. The First Peoples respect the bear and call it an elder kinsman. The bear is the protector of the animal kingdom.

Beaver

Two great square cutting teeth and a cross-hatched tail identify the beaver crest. Sometimes it has ears and a small nose. The beaver often carries a small stick in her front paws. The first beaver was a woman with brown hair who refused to come out of a lake. She grew soft brown fur on her body, and her apron turned into a tail.

Eagle

In an eagle crest, the beak has a strong curve, but is not hooked. It is usually open, with a tongue, and is shorter than the raven's beak. The head has a crest ear form, which is not curled; wings, tail, and claws are often shown. The eagle is a powerful crest; even the feathers have power. Eagle down is used in many ceremonies to honour people, welcome strangers, and promote peace.

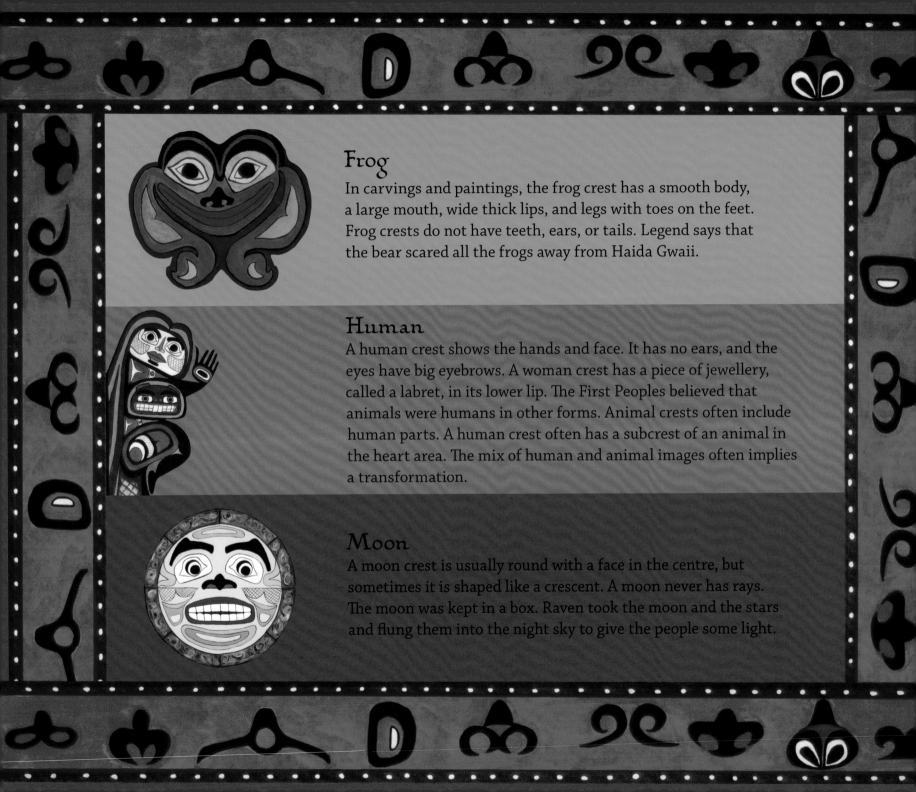

Frog

In carvings and paintings, the frog crest has a smooth body, a large mouth, wide thick lips, and legs with toes on the feet. Frog crests do not have teeth, ears, or tails. Legend says that the bear scared all the frogs away from Haida Gwaii.

Human

A human crest shows the hands and face. It has no ears, and the eyes have big eyebrows. A woman crest has a piece of jewellery, called a labret, in its lower lip. The First Peoples believed that animals were humans in other forms. Animal crests often include human parts. A human crest often has a subcrest of an animal in the heart area. The mix of human and animal images often implies a transformation.

Moon

A moon crest is usually round with a face in the centre, but sometimes it is shaped like a crescent. A moon never has rays. The moon was kept in a box. Raven took the moon and the stars and flung them into the night sky to give the people some light.

Mosquito

A mosquito crest has a long narrow nose with many teeth. It has wings and small clawlike feet. Legend says that the mosquito was once a giant monster. An angry mother pushed it into a bonfire and destroyed it. But the sparks from the fire turned into thousands of mosquitoes.

Owl

The owl crest always has large eyes and a small sharp beak. Pointed ear shapes are often shown. Because the owl can fly soundlessly in the dark, the First Peoples endow the owl with magic powers and wisdom. They believe that when an owl flies overhead, someone in the village will die. When people were in great need, the shamans would call to the owl for help.

Raven

A long straight beak, often holding the sun, identifies a raven crest. The raven will have wings, a tail, and claws. The raven is full of mystical powers. He is a transformer, a hero, and a trickster. He can turn himself into anything, anytime. He released the sun, moon, and stars from a wooden box. The raven is black because he flew too close to the sun and was scorched and blackened with soot.

Salmon

The salmon crest has a hooked jaw, panels of red flesh, and, often, red eggs in the belly. Because the salmon comes back to the same location every year, the First Peoples of the Pacific Northwest did not have to travel very far from home to augment their food sources. The salmon is called *kiyotala*. Any set of twins can claim the salmon as their crest.

Sun

The sun crest is round with a face in the middle. It has rays, which vary in length and detail. The sun always walks from the east to sleep in his lodge in the west. The sun never stops to listen to people, who always want more sunshine. If it did, its light would evaporate the clouds, the earth would overheat, and the forests would burn.

Wolf

A wolf crest shows a long muzzle with flared nostrils, sharp fangs, a curled tail, and large ears. The wolf can see in the dark and run great distances. Legend says that the wolf got lost and began to howl in despair. A woman looking for her lost son found the wolf instead and took him to her lodge. He still howls when the moon is full, hoping his brothers will find him.

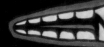
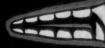

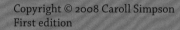

Heritage House Publishing Company Ltd.

#108 – 17665 66A Avenue
Surrey, BC V3S 2A7
www.heritagehouse.ca

PO Box 468
Custer, WA
98240-0468

Library and Archives Canada Cataloguing in Publication

Simpson, Caroll, 1951–
    The first beaver / written and illustrated by Caroll Simpson.

ISBN 978-1-894974-50-9

    1. Beavers—Juvenile fiction. 2. Indians of North America—Northwest Coast of North America—Juvenile fiction. I. Title.

PS8637.I484F57 2008   jC813'6   C2008-902379-X

Library of Congress Control Number: 2008930358

Edited by Grenfell Featherstone
Book design by R-House Design

Heritage House acknowledges the financial support for its publishing program from the Government of Canada through the Book Publishing Industry Development Program (BPIDP), Canada Council for the Arts and the British Columbia Arts Council.

Canada Council
for the Arts
Conseil des Arts
du Canada

BRITISH COLUMBIA
ARTS COUNCIL

Printed and bound in China

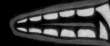